CORNELL DYER AND THE HOWLS OF BASKETVILLE

An *Adventures of Cornell Dyer* supernatural mystery

Denise M. Baran-Unland

In collaboration with
Timothy M. Baran

Illustrated by Sue Midlock

This book is lovingly dedicated to the reader, whoever you might be.

"The world is full of obvious things which nobody by any chance ever observes."

— *Sir Arthur Conan Doyle, The Hound of the Baskervilles*

CONTENTS

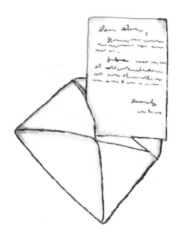

PROLOGUE

Supernatural super sleuth Cornell Dyer was saying good-bye to the janitor when a student rushed up and rudely interrupted.

"Mr. Janitor, have you seen the world famous supernatural super sleuth Cornell Dyer?" the student panted.

"I'm right here," Cornell said. "I am he who specializes in Amulets, Fortune-Telling (with and without cards), Ghost-Hunting, Horoscopes, Numerology, Palm-Reading, Potions, Séances, Spells, Vampire-Slaying, controlling zambicallo populations, and deactivating Moravian pink goblins, cold whispers, and classroom skeletons with..."

"You have a letter!"

Cornell snatched the envelope, ripped it open, and read:

My dearest Professor,

I have been looking for you for a long time.

I had to use the last of my magic in a bottle to find you.

Please come with haste for I am running out of time. An old haunt has returned.

I have not seen it, but I can feel it. I feel it lurking in the dark shadows around unsuspecting corners.

A coldness comes at night that leaves the grass frosted and dead.

I hear it. The faint howls grow stronger in the night.

I have stayed where I've been all these years protecting the thing that needs protecting but now, more than ever I am in need of a pair of hands.

There is a door, and behind the door is a hallway. It's windowless and dark and all manner of wicked creatures move about stopping me from advancing. This hallway has never known light.

We must join together again. One must survive if the others fails.

My dear man Wipston is with me. We are preparing for our last mystery.

Please join us my friend.

"For by the moonlight we dance,

"And from fingertips flow romance,

"Like a river springing to life,

"The dogs snarl and bite,

"To keep her safe at night,

"But even still there is no chance,

"For the darkness buries the day,

"The priests forget how to pray,

"And the ground shakes with the souls of the dead,

"The schoolteacher weeps,

"For the husband she seeks,

"That man who went off to war,

"He left with a grin,

"Spread over his chin,

"To be seen nevermore."

He is coming.

Sherman A. Homes

Cornell pushed past the student and ran from the room. His substitute teaching days were over.
Finally!

CHAPTER ONE: SHADIER THAN A FOREST

Cornell scowled as he recklessly veered his large motor home off the highway and onto Route Nanoc Elyod, still clutching Sherman Homes' crumpled letter in one hand.

Now this wasn't the first time Cornell drove onto hidden roads with strange names. Cornell had been a supernatural super sleuth for a very long time. He wasn't daunted by the unusual and mysterious.

No, Cornell was scowling because he was driving in Michigan.

Again.

Why, with all the places Cornell

traveled to solve supernatural mysteries, why did he always wind up in Michigan?

Again!

Just wait until Cornell caught up with Sherman Homes.

Just wait.

After all the mysteries Cornell helped Sherman solve!

Cornell thought about "The Sign of Three Times Three," where nine ghosts terrorized anyone who owned pearl necklaces. The ghosts ransacked jewelry boxes while the owners slept and removed just one pearl from each necklace. This left the necklaces unwearable until Cornell and Sherman solved the mystery.

Cornell thought about "The Green-Headed League," where ghost Martians were digging trenches beneath grocery stores and stealing food to bring back to Mars, where no food grew. This left lots of people hungry until Cornell and Sherman solved the mystery.

Cornell thought about, "The Mystery of the Cardboard Refrigerator Box," where ice ghosts stole new refrigerators to sell as new homes to other ice ghosts. When people walked into their kitchen for a snack, they found a cardboard refrigerator box where the refrigerator should be. This also left lots of people hungry until Cornell and Sherman solved the mystery.

Each of these supernatural mysteries happened in Michigan. Why?

Michigan!

Arrrghh!

He swerved onto Lawrence Lane, the road that led directly to Basketville. He zoomed past an abandoned factory, which sat right on the edge of the Forest of Fear.

Cornell snorted at the name: Forest of Fear. Oooh, he was so afraid!

Cornell passed the old train depot and drove bumpity-bump over the old tracks. No one had used the depot and the tracks for years, not since a train had gone through the tunnel and never came out. At least, that's what the old story said. But the story was older than Cornell. Who knew if it were true?

He tossed the letter behind him. Sherman always wrote such overly dramatic letters. Why couldn't he simply write, "Help me solve this mystery. It concerns dogs. Maybe, werewolves."

Was that so hard???

Cornell screeched onto Bakery Drive. Then he slowed the motor home, scanning for Sherman's address as he rolled down the street.

The run-down bungalows were tightly packed and looked like one low house. Cornell also rolled past skeletal timbers and tall weeds, where thugs probably had torched bungalows.

As Cornell drove, he noted leaking roofs, rusty fences, cracked windows, missing shingles, peeling paint, unraked leaves, overgrown yards, and crumbling sidewalks.

He noted people lurking in shadows.

He noted people peeping through curtains.

He noted people selling stolen roast beef sandwiches on the street corners. He noted their winks, covert glances, and quickly pocketed dimes.

Cornell's mouth watered, and he licked his lips. Cornell was very hungry from his very long drive, and he loved a good roast beef sandwich. But supernatural super sleuths worth their salt did not buy stolen roast beef sandwiches, no matter how fresh and tasty those sandwiches looked. Because if a supernatural super sleuth ever ate a stolen roast beef sandwich...

He slammed on the brakes. 122 Bakery Drive. This was the place.

Cornell shut off the engine and grabbed orange drinks from under his seat. Then he eased onto the ground, shoving orange drinks into every pocket of his colorful patchwork blazer.

This mystery better be worth it, he thought.

Michigan! Ugh!

Cornell lumbered to the crooked gate and lifted the latch; the gate CREAKED backward, as usual.

He crossed the yard, scarcely larger than a pocket handkerchief today. Very strange.

He trotted up three broken concrete steps to the slanted and pitted concrete porch.

The torn screen door hung by a rusty hinge. Cornell carefully opened it and banged on the old wooden door. Then he dug his fists deeply into his blue jean pockets and waited for Sherman Homes.

But nothing happened.

So Cornell banged again.

And Cornell waited some more.

Cornell banged.

And waited.

He BANGED and BANGED! and BANGED!!!

Nothing.

Eureka!

Cornell remembered Sherman Homes kept a key behind the bulb under the front porch light, except – the porch light was gone and so was the key. So he jiggled the doorknob and peered through dusty glass, hoping to glimpse Sherman. But the shades were drawn.

Grumbling, Cornell sat on the porch and opened the first orange drink. He sipped and waited for Sherman to appear.

Cornell sipped and watched the bright afternoon sun sink toward the horizon.

Cornell sipped and watched twilight turn the dismal scene to gray.

Cornell sipped and peered into the darkness. Shivering, he pulled his blazer over his stained T-shirt and barreled chest. He ran a hand through his dirty black curls. He sighed loud, irritable sighs.

Finally he trudged to the motor home for his little black transistor radio. He went back to the porch and tuned into his favorite station. He opened another orange drink and hummed to his favorite Wagnerian opera.

He thought of the words of Professor Christine Lucille BeckmanShire. Christine helped him solve the zambie mystery at Paradise Falls.

"When the sun disappears below the horizon, and the birds stop singing their daily song, and the owls and other night creatures start roaming the earth," Christine had said.

So Cornell knew the time was eight-fifteen. Where was Sherman Homes?

Just then, the door popped open. He heard a very familiar, very pleasant voice. "Professor Cornell Dyer! How nice to see you!"

Then the man, Dr. Jim Wipston, called over his shoulder, "Sherman, Cornell Dyer is here!"

Cornell leaped up, knocking a dozen orange drink cans off the stoop in his hurry and anger.

"Nice to see me! Nice to see me! I

knocked and knocked! Why didn't you answer?"

A very calm, very refined voice called out from inside the house: "My dear, Dr. Wipston! What is Cornell doing on the stoop?"

"That's 'professor' to you!" Cornell shouted right back.

But Dr. Wipston, a very elegant gray-haired man in a gray, three-piece suit, called over his shoulder, "I cannot make that deduction, Sherman. I merely stepped out for the mail."

With that, Dr. Wipston lifted the lid on an old, dented mailbox and withdrew a dozen envelopes.

"Well, please invite Cornell in!" Sherman was still hidden within the house. "It's not safe to be sitting outside in this neighborhood at night. He should come inside and get warm."

"Then you should have answered the door!" Cornell yelled.

"Did you knock?" Dr. Wipston asked kindly.

"Yes! I knocked and knocked and knocked!"

"Well, we don't answer knocks. We only

answer doorbells. Didn't you read the sign?"

"What sign???"

Dr. Wipston pointed to the old, large, very ornate doorknob. So Cornell stiffly got on his knees and looked.

Underneath the knob, on the tiniest slip of paper, about one hundredth the size of a postage stamp were the following words written with spidery penmanship:

Ring bell.

"How was I supposed to see that?" Cornell complained as he struggled to his feet.

Dr. Wipston smiled a lofty smile. "You are a supernatural super sleuth, aren't you? And you know Sherman is a consulting supernatural super sleuth, don't you? Then you should know that..."

"...that it's just another one of Sherman's 'small' rules," Cornell rudely interrupted.

Cornell was ready to leave the porch, solve the mystery, and find the best hamburger stand in town, even if the stand sold stolen hamburgers.

Dr. Wipston smiled again. "We don't answer knocks. Please follow me."

Cornell stepped through the doorway into a small parlor. He didn't remove his dirty, worn sneakers. He noted one sagging couch and one stained armchair on the threadbare carpet.

He noted an old console television, screen missing, against a wall.

He noted a plastic spider plant in a scuffed plastic bucket in the corner.

He noted two photos on the wall, held in place by yellowed, crackling cellophane tape: Sherman Homes' fourth grade class photo and Dr. Wipston's certificate of doctory.

The small parlor merged with a small dining room. Cornell noted a large oak table with a tattered lace cloth, set for eight.

He noted dishes thick with dust.

He noted silverware green with tarnish.

He noted a small bathroom left of the dining room and closed door at the dining room's far end.

All the same – so far.

Dr. Wipston opened the door and

Cornell walked across the squeaking boards into a small square kitchen.

Cornell noted an old small square table and three old wooden chairs.

Cornell noted a refrigerator and stove from the 1930s.

Cornell noted a large porcelain sink with a hand pump.

Cornell noted homemade wooden cabinets with chipped white paint.

But a pot simmered merrily on the range and savory smells filled the air, Cornell's favorite part of the kitchen.

"This way, Professor," Dr. Wipston said.

Dr. Wipston opened a closet door on the left, which opened into a long, narrow hallway, much longer than the length of the house. Cornell followed Dr. Wipston down the long, long hallway to its end.

Dr. Wipston stopped and gestured to a door on his left.

"I'll leave you to speak with Sherman," Dr. Wipston said. "I must check on dinner.

CHAPTER TWO: MIDNIGHT ESCAPADE

Sherman Homes was a tall, thin man, much than taller than Cornell and way, way thinner. His eyes were brown yet piercing. His brown curls were clean and nicely brushed, unlike Cornell's on both counts.

He sat in a tall leather wingback chair in the middle of the study across from the fireplace, where a cheery fire crackled away. He wore black silk trousers, warm brown slippers, and a royal blue smoking jacket.

Cornell wore faded blue jeans, his patchwork quilt, dirty sneakers, last week's socks, and a blue T-shirt that read, "Your Ghost is Toast."

As Cornell stood there, he noted nothing had changed since his last visit. He noted the same leatherbound books on bookshelves on two walls.

He noted the same bay window with a majestic view of the sun setting over the plains. He noted a window seat with a velvet cushion below the window.

He noted a bearskin rug in front of the fireplace.

He noted enormous chandeliers hanging from the tall ceilings, their lights dimmed for comfort and rest.

Classical piano music played from the quadrophonic stereo. The aroma of a mouthwatering roasted pheasant wafted into the room.

Sherman steadily doodled with a fine pencil in a softcover book, about the size of a coloring book, which lay across his lap. Sherman also blew blue bubbles from his blue plastic bubble pipe and sipped grape soda. The little square ice cubes inside the glass tinkled pleasantly.

Cornell wondered if Sherman were passing the time or solving a mystery. For Sherman saw mysteries where mysteries didn't exist.

Like the time Sherman found a stray sock in the house.

Sherman had grabbed his magnifying glass and searched high and low for the missing person – until Dr. Wipston arrived with the laundry basket, the sock's mate dangling over the edge.

Or the time Sherman found a dozen shoes scattered beneath the clothesline.

Sherman scoured the neighborhood for the missing people – until Dr. Wipston arrived and pointed to the children running barefoot races in the next yard.

Or the time Sherman discovered seven white mugs in the kitchen cabinet and wondered what band of thieves stole the eighth mug.

As Sherman organized a search party, Dr. Wipston walked into the room, sipping black coffee from the eighth white mug.

Or the time the kitchen table jiggled.

Sherman researched all tables in the world to see if their legs were getting shorter, too – until Dr. Wipston strolled into the room with a screwdriver and tightened the leg.

This is the way Dr. Wipston once explained it. If a string were hanging off a sweater, Cornell would examine the string for ways to cheaply mass produce vampire slaying sweaters; Sherman would examine the string for signs of foul play; and Dr. Wipston would cut the string and wear the sweater.

"My dear, Cornell, you should have rung the doorbell, especially with all the terror running around these days." Sherman did not look up. "It's not safe."

"Don't care," Cornell retorted. "I knocked and knocked. You should have answered the knocks."

Sherman kept doodling. "My dear, Cornell. We don't answer knocks." He glanced up. "And we did leave you a clue."

"You didn't!"

Sherman shrugged. "Oh. Well, I thought we left a clue." He looked Cornell up and down. "You've gained a few pounds. You eat too many potato chips, my friend."

Dr. Wipston appeared in the doorway. "Dinner is nearly ready. Professor, your room is directly off this study." He motioned toward a narrow hall beyond the study's door. "You may leave your suitcase in there."

Cornell snorted. "I'll stay in the motor home. This mystery won't take long to..."

"Nonsense." Sherman returned to his doodling. "We insist. Hurry and get your suitcase. It's not nice out there this time of night."

"You're sure you'll let me back inside?"

Dr. Wipston smiled. "Just ring the bell."

Cornell stomped out of the house and onto the porch – and paused at the eerie change.

The people were gone.

A light wind riffled through the leaves.

The air crackled with electricity. Cornell's neck and scalp prickled.

He flew down the steps and into the motor home, eager to pack up and get back inside. As he rummaged through piles of dirty laundry, he caught a glimpse through his window of Sherman opening the screen door and peering into the night. Sherman looked left and right and cocked his head, as if listening hard.

Cornell quickly stuffed dirty clothes into a garbage bag and snatched his overnight sleuthing kit from under the couch. He dumped a few orange drinks and oversized candy bars on top. He didn't grab any soap or shampoo. Saturday was bath tonight. Today was only Monday.

Then Cornell dashed out of the motor home and ran up the now empty porch. Obediently, he rang the bell.

Dr. Wipston promptly opened the door and led Cornell through the parlor, the dining room, the kitchen, the study, and into Cornell's room.

"We waited dinner for you." Dr. Wipston smiled warmly. "Please leave your bag and join us."

What a shabby room! Cornell almost fled to his comfortable motor home. But he didn't. A supernatural super sleuth must endure many hardships when solving supernatural mysteries.

Besides, if Cornell left, he'd miss dinner.

He sighed and noted none of the comforts in Sherman's study.

Instead, Cornell noted white walls yellowed with age.

He noted the chipped white radiator leaning precariously against the far wall.

He noted an old, scuffed bureau opposite an old, sagging brass bed, covered with a faded twill bedspread.

He noted missing slats on the window shades and the gloom of the dark backyard.

He noted a large box marked **CORNELL DYER** sat in the middle of the room.

"Eureka!" Cornell cried.

He dropped to his knees and opened the flaps. He found empty orange drink cans, expired potato chip bags, a broken flashlight, candy bar wrappers, and frayed shoelaces.

"You left those behind," Dr. Wipston said from the doorway. "Do take them this time. Let's eat now, shall we?"

Cornell leaped to his feet.

They crowded around the little square kitchen table, their knees touching as they ate. They passed dish after savory dish: juicy pheasant, garlicky roast beef, sage and onion stuffing, buttery mashed potatoes with rivers of hot gravy, warm fluffy crescent rolls, crisp lettuce salad and relish trays, and three large pies for dessert: cherry, pecan, and pumpkin.

As Cornell cut into his third slice of pie, he asked, "So what's the mystery?"

Sherman reached into his back pocket and set the coloring book on the table. "Open it."

Cornell did, his mouth very full of pie. He flipped through the pages. This wasn't a coloring book. It was a connect-the-dot book.

"Jim and I have worked on this mystery for a long time." Sherman reached for his water goblet. "I've finally connected the dots."

"Connected the dots!" Cornell shouted. "Connected the dots! What about the mystery?"

"Look closely, Professor," Dr. Wipston said while buttering another roll. "What do you see?"

Cornell looked closer and stuffed another forkful of cherry pie into his mouth.

"It's a map," Sherman cried impatiently. "It's a map of Basketville. And right here," Sherman pointed on number thirty-two. "Right here is where I lost the scent." He closed the book and folded his arms. "That's why Jim and I fed you well. We go to work tonight."

Cornell yawned loudly. "Can't we solve the mystery in the morning?"

"No, we must search at night," Sherman said. "We've been following the tail – er- trail…"

Dr. Wipston chuckled at Sherman's forced little joke.

"…of these howls," Sherman continued. "We must take this map and search street by street, all the way to the Forest of Fear. We must be very sure we are right on track."

"We're looking for dogs?" Cornell sneered.

Sherman's eyes flashed. He opened his mouth to retort, but Dr. Wipston held up his hand.

"Let me explain, Sherman," Dr. Wipston said. "You see, Professor, two months ago, strange things started to happen."

"What kind of things?" Cornell demanded.

"Howling things," Dr. Wipston said. "At midnight. At two in the morning."

"A dog's howl?"

Dr. Wipston frowned. "No, not a dog's howl. Please pay attention, Professor."

"A werewolf?" Cornell snickered.

"No werewolves!" Sherman shouted

impatiently. "Now listen! Wherever the howl is closest, people and objects disappear."

"People go for a walk and lose their keys?"

"Sometimes," Dr. Wipston set his napkin next to his plate and looked evenly at Cornell. "Sometimes entire neighborhoods disappear."

Cornell laughed. "This neighborhood should disappear! All of Michigan should disappear!"

"So with three of us," Dr. Jim Wipston continued, ignoring Cornell's rude remarks, "we can get near the howl, corner it, and learn more."

Cornell stretched hard and yawned very loudly. "Why do you need me?"

"If something happens to one of us, only one will remain," Dr. Wipston leaned forward. His eyes looked stern. "It will be hard for one to carry on. Three is better than two. If one disappears, two can work together to solve the mystery."

Cornell yawned even more loudly, not even bothering to cover his mouth. He was a supernatural super sleuth, an expert at solving the most challenging supernatural mysteries. If Sherman Homes and Dr. Wipston wanted to pay him lots of money to chase a dog, who was he to argue?

He stood and stretched again. "I'm taking a nap first."

"Leave the light on," Dr. Wipston advised.

"Sure," Cornell said.

Soon Cornell was lying in bed, blankets to his chin, and giving the lamp chain a gentle tug. The room plunged into darkness, and Cornell fell asleep.

GONG!!!

Cornell bolted upright in bed.

The room was sweltering.

His wet T-shirt stuck to his chest.

His damp curls stuck to his forehead.

The blanket was wrapped around him.

He yanked it back, slid out of bed, and wandered barefoot into the empty study, absently scratching his arm. A long wall clock read eleven forty-five.

He wandered into the empty kitchen and heard voices from the dining room. He opened the door and peered inside.

Sherman and Dr. Wipston leaned over

the dining room table in full, matching tactical gear: creased pants, rugged boots, armor, and shields. With heads together, they talked softly as they traced the routes on the maps, They checked and rechecked their magical weapons and instruments, which they took from the table in perfect synchronization and hooked them here and stuffed them in a disappearing pocket there.

Cornell caught snatches of conversation:

"What time shall we…?"

"Who's going left at the…?"

"What's the signal if we meet danger at…?"

"If you need me, call this…"

Cornell cleared his voice. Both men looked at him, looked at each other, and looked at Cornell again, frowning in disapproval.

"Hurry and get ready," Dr. Wipston urged. "We must leave soon."

Cornell gave a long yawn. He staggered to his room for his shoes and socks. He hunted for his patchwork blazer and found it twisted in the blanket. He put it on and checked he still had duct tape. He plodded to the dining room, completely forgetting his overnight sleuthing kit, still sitting on the old bureau. Sherman and Dr. Wipston had rolled up the maps. They slid into long overcoats and added matching fedoras. Sherman wore brown. Dr. Wipston wore gray.

They glanced at Cornell and then at each other again. But Dr. Wipston only said, "Let's go."

Cornell reached for the light, but Dr. Wipston said, "Leave the light on, Professor. Please."

With a shrug, Cornell followed his friends out the front door and into the darkness.

They walked single file down Bakery Drive, with Sherman confidently leading the way, occasionally glancing this way and that way with his sharp, ever-attentive eyes. They passed one dilapidated house after another in a night ominously still and empty of life. Cornell saw not one thug.

"Strange," Cornell said aloud.

"What's strange?" Dr. Wipston asked.

"No thugs. Are they afraid of the dark?"

Dr. Wipston nodded. "They are very

afraid."

Cornell snickered.

"What's so funny?" Dr. Wipston asked.

"Figures scaredy cat thugs live in Michigan."

Dr. Wipston did not smile.

Sherman turned right onto Cookery Drive, left onto Muffin Lane, and then right onto Focaccia Avenue, and then left onto Range Road, and then right onto Cake Court. They proceeded to the end, passed between two houses, and strolled directly into the Forest of Fear. Sherman abruptly stopped and spun around.

"We split up here." Sherman handed Cornell a small square metal box. It looked like a transistor radio, but Cornell knew better. But then, Cornell was a supernatural super sleuth. Supernatural super sleuths stayed up to date with their devices.

"Now remember," Sherman warned. "Radio immediately if you..."

"If – what?" Cornell asked.

Dr. Wipston placed his hand on Cornell's shoulder in a reassuring way. "If – anything."

"Cornell, go left."

Sherman pointed, and Cornell fumed. What an insult! Cornell knew which direction was left. Sherman didn't need to point.

"Jim, go right. I'll go straight. Depart!"

Grumbling, Cornell headed deeper into the woods, groping for his ghost flashlight. A ghost flashlight is a powerful instrument. It lights up the way as bright as daylight but is undetectable by any creature – live or dead.

As he strolled along, Cornell whistled under his breath, still annoyed. The world's three most amazing supernatural super sleuths were wasting their keen, amazing talents chasing a howl in the middle of a forest at midnight when they should be tucked into their beds sleeping.

Far in the distance, Cornell sensed a faint, very undoglike howl. He stopped to listen.

Nothing.

He cocked his head.

Nothing.

A hard jab in the small of his back knocked him flat, a shadow streaked past. Cornell fumbled for his radio; he heard Dr, Wipston's faint shouts.

Cornell jumped up and sprinted to the

center of the forest, near the opening, and bumped into Sherman, gasping for breath.

Dr. Wipston sped from the trees. "It's a trap! It's a trap!"

He fell to his knees and whipped something out of his pocket. "Stand back!"

Sherman grabbed Cornell's arm and ran.

A BANG flung Cornell into a tree; a burst of light blinded him; the earth shook beneath him; a black mist rose before him; and sharp teeth clamped onto his leg.

CHAPTER THREE: THE CAMERA CANNOT LIE

"Come on!" Dr. Jim Wipston shouted.

Sherman pulled Cornell to his feet and raced out of the forest after Dr, Wipston. They never stopped running until they cleared Cake Court and returned to Range Road.

"What happened?" Cornell panted once they slowed their steps and caught their breaths.

"The thing lured us in there," Dr. Wipston said. "It wanted us to split up all along."

"So splitting up was a bad idea?" Cornell huffed as he limped.

"It was the best idea," Sherman said, completely unruffled. "Now we know for sure."

"What do we know?" Cornell demanded. "And what did Jim do back there?"

"I chased it off with light," Dr. Wipston said mildly. "Things that live in darkness shun light, so I...Cornell! What happened to your leg?"

Cornell glanced at his right leg. His jeans were shredded. His leg had a gaping, bleeding crater.

"That's why I removed the lightbulb from the front porch lamp," Sherman said haughtily. "To draw it close – but not too close. We don't turn off lights in the house at night. Light protects us." He yawned and patted his mouth. "At any rate, we won't solve the mystery tonight. Bedtime!"

"Stop!" Dr. Wipston grabbed Sherman's arm.

Of course, Sherman stopped immediately and so did Cornell. Dr. Wipston sat on the sidewalk, rolled up Cornell's tattered jeans, and carefully examined Cornell's wounded leg.

"It's a bad bite." Dr. Wipston said. "I

must operate."

"What - now?" Sherman asked in astonishment. "I'm ready for sleep." He yawned again to prove his point.

"Me, too." Cornell yawned even harder.

Cornell only wanted to crawl into bed. Dr. Wipston could operate in the morning, after Cornell had a good night's sleep and a hearty breakfast.

"Yes, now." Dr. Wipston started removing items from all the pockets of his perfectly creased trousers. He laid them in an even row on the concrete. "Unless you want Cornell to die on this sidewalk."

"Well, that would be hard to explain, I guess," Sherman admitted, but he didn't sound happy about it.

"Sit, Professor," Dr. Wipston said.

Cornell, too tired to protest, obediently sat.

Dr. Wipston carefully cut Cornell's pant leg away with protective scissors to better access the wound. Any supernatural super sleuth knows what protective scissors are. Protective scissors are very safe. They only cut things that need cutting.

Dr. Wipston then cleaned Cornell's

wound with Johnny-On-The-Spot Surgical Cleansing Gel. He poured You Name It, I Get Rid of It all-purpose germ killing powder. Then Dr. Wipston took his magic needle, threaded it with magical suture thread, and stitched Cornell's wound closed faster than Cornell could say, "Jack rabbit" or "lickety-split."

Not that Cornell said either of those. He was bone-tired, and his leg throbbed hard.

"There," Dr. Wipston said after he cleaned his tools, returned them to the correct pockets, and helped Cornell up. "Your leg will be sore for a few days. But then you'll be good as new."

The entire process only took five minutes. But Sherman rudely and impatiently tapped his foot the entire time.

"Are you quite done?" he demanded.

"Quite." Dr. Wipston smiled a weary smile. "Let's go home."

Dawn was lighting the sky with pink streaks by the time the three tired sleuths returned to 122 Bakery Drive.

Cornell heard a dog, a regular dog, bark.

He heard birds twitter.

He heard an engine roar to life.

"Shut up!" Cornell yelled.

No one argued with him.

They stumbled up the front steps and into the house. They quickly splashed away their surface grime in the kitchen sink. They poured some quick bowls of cold cereal and milk.

"Leave the light on," Dr. Wipston warned.

Then they slunk to their bedrooms.

Cornell fell asleep after he switched off the light and his head hit the pillow. But it was a horrible, nightmarish sleep, full of shadows, sharp biting teeth, and wheezing, menacing howls that slipped into his mind, and ...

He bolted up in the dark, a dark that was too dark for early morning. His heart pounded; he heard unearthly howling in his ears. He switched on the lamp and took a couple of deep breaths.

The howling stopped.

Cornell folded a pillow over his head to block out the light. Then he rolled over, the mattress jostling beneath him, the springs giving a firm and annoying SQUEAK!

And the bed repeated those squeaks with each breath in and out.

SQUEAK!   SQUEAK!   SQUEAK! SQUEAK!

Cornell angrily flung back the covers and slid out of bed. He rummaged in his blazer for his supersonic, fix-a-squeak screwdriver but couldn't find it. He searched every pocket. He held the blazer upside down and shook it hard. Out tumbled half-eaten candy bars, French fry wrappers, old mayonnaise packets, a pair of enchanted hares, three blind mice, and half a dozen telephone devices resembling billfolds.

No screwdriver.

He sighed irritably and stamped his foot.

It probably fell out when that – thing – knocked him to the ground in the forest. Well, maybe he had a spare in his box of leftovers.

Three minutes later, the box's contents were strewn over the floor, and Cornell still didn't have a screwdriver. Maybe he had one in his overnight sleuthing bag.

But the overnight sleuthing bag wasn't

on top of the old bureau. Did it fall? Cornell looked on one side and the other. He even pushed the heavy piece of furniture out of the way.

Nothing.

He paused to scratch his head.

Very strange, he thought.

Had he returned the overnight sleuthing kit to the motor home and simply forgot? Well, no matter. He'd look for a screwdriver somewhere else.

Cornell hobbled out of his room, through the brightly lit hall, and into the brightly lit kitchen.

Daylight seeped through the tightly closed blinds. The bright ceiling lights and all the table lamps were still turned on.

Bits and smears of last night's feast strewed the kitchen table.

The counter was full of dirty pots and pans and magical weapons and instruments.

His mind swirling with fatigue, Cornell opened the first drawer: flatware.

He opened the second drawer: measuring cups and spoons.

He opened the third drawer: butcher knives, boning knives, paring knives, utility knives, steak knives.

He opened the fourth drawer: pens, pencils, markers, twist ties, cable ties, and a pencil case with the label: KEEP OUT.

So naturally Cornell unzipped it. But he only found a note in tiny letters: I said, KEEP OUT!

He slammed the drawer. Maybe he could find a screwdriver in the basement.

He opened the back door, which led to a mudroom brightly lit by a single powerful bulb and steep basement stairs. He grabbed the handrail for balance (since his leg was throbbing very hard now), and inched his way down, down, down, down, down to the bottom.

It was a musty, low-ceilinged basement, the kind where a very tall man must duck. He noted open rafters and gray flaking paint on the concrete walls and floors. Cornell easily noted this because every electric bulb brightly shone through the antique wall lanterns.

Cornell also noted an old furnace, an old water heater, an old washer and dryer, and an old workbench made of old boards and old, rusty nails.

He noted an open crawl space filled

with two feet of old gravel.

He noted old spiders on old spider webs and old beetle-like creatures scuttling past on old teeny tiny feet.

He dragged his wounded leg to the workbench and rummaged around the old toolchests, opening drawers and tossing items aside.

Cornell didn't find a single screwdriver. But he found another box marked "CORNELL DYER."

That's "professor" to them, he thought crossly as he ripped off the tape. Maybe THIS box had a screwdriver, so Cornell could silence the squeak and FINALLY get back to sleep.

Fifteen minutes later, Cornell was quaffing his second expired orange drink and sorting through the dead batteries, dirty socks, a cracked belt that no longer fit him, and expired packets of all-purpose potion powder. Scattered at the bottom were several old sleuthing photographs from old mysteries he solved with Sherman and Dr. Wipston in their early sleuthing years.

Cornell shuffled through the photos, smiling weary half-smiles here and there at the happy memories of their previous successes.

Then his heart nearly stopped.

He held up the last photo for a closer look.

Cornell himself had taken it on the front porch of 122 Bakery Drive. Cornell clearly recalled that day, at least twenty years ago. Sherman's uncle, a world traveler, had stopped by the house with a failed time machine, his birthday gift to Sherman.

So they sat on the porch together – Sherman, Dr. Wipston. and Sherman's Uncle Teabody – so Cornell could snap the historic photo.

Now it wasn't the photo that troubled Cornell. It was the smudge in the bottom right.

The smudge was faint and wispy, so faint and wispy and hairlike that only a trained supernatural super sleuth with a trained supernatural sleuthing eye could detect it.

But detect it Cornell did.

And at that moment, Cornell knew.

The thing they sought wasn't new.

It had been here all along.

CHAPTER FOUR: SHADOWS AND WISPS

Cornell sprinted up the stairs, photo in hand, and bumped into Dr. Wipston, who was sleepily raising shades and switching off lights.

"What are you doing?" Cornell screamed.

He ran through rooms, turning lights back on.

"My dear Cornell." Dr. Wipston grabbed Cornell by his shoulders as he ran past. "What is the matter with you?"

Cornell waved the photograph. "It's here! It's here! It's been here all along!"

"Do make him shut up!" Sherman called from a far part of the house. "I'm trying to sleep!"

"Get over here now!" Cornell roared.

Dr. Wipston took the photo from Cornell's hand and studied it, looking troubled. Then set the photo on the kitchen table and reached for the tea kettle. Sherman stumbled into the room, glowering and rubbing his eyes.

"Can't you let a sleuth get his rest?" Sherman complained. "We have a mystery to solve!"

Cornell snatched the photo and shoved it near Sherman's face. "Look at this!"

Sherman looked. He turned pale.

"How can this be?" Sherman murmured. "This photo is twenty years old."

"At least," Dr. Wipston added.

"Do you see?" Cornell shouted.

"The...thing...is in the house!"

The tea kettle whistled. Dr. Wipston calmly poured three cups and set them on the table among last night's dirty dishes.

"It's not in the house," Dr. Wipston said, unruffled. "We keep the lights on. Let's discuss this new finding over tea. Then I'll make breakfast."

They sat at the table for nearly an hour, sipping cup after cup of hot tea and not talking.

Sherman turned to a fresh page in his book and slowly connected dots with his fine pen.

Finally Dr. Wipston broke the silence. "Sherman, are you thinking what I'm thinking?"

Sherman nodded. "We were wrong about its first appearance."

"Aren't you worried?" Cornell demanded.

"Of course, I'm worried," Sherman shot back. "It means my calculations are incorrect."

"Calculations!" Cornell stuck out his leg. "Your 'calculations' cost me a chomp to the bone!"

"Pshaw." Sherman returned to his book. "Stop making a fuss. Jim fixed you up nicely."

On cue, Dr. Wipston rose, unbuttoning his cuffs and rolling up his sleeves. "I'll wash the dishes and cook breakfast. Professor, please clear the dining room table. You may set the dusty dishes on the sideboard."

An hour later, Dr. Wipston was serving Eggs Benedict, Belgium waffles with warm maple syrup, Potatoes O'Brien, and freshly squeezed orange juice. They ate at the kitchen table again, knees touching again, because Sherman insisted.

"Why did I clear the table?" Cornell groused as he scooped hearty fourth helpings onto his plate.

"For the work," Sherman said in a tone suggesting Cornell should know better. "You really are tiresome first thing in the morning."

Cornell's eyes strayed to the wall clock. It was past one o'clock in the afternoon. Whatever.

Finally Dr. Wipston said, "Sherman, are you ready?"

Sherman met his eyes and closed the book.

"Then let's bring the albums," Dr. Wipston said. "Cornell, please help us carry them to the dining room table."

They spent another hour removing all the photograph albums from all the shelves in every part of the house and lugging them into the dining room. They stacked them on the table, leaving room for "the work," as Sherman said, and they stacked them on every space of the floor and against the walls.

Armed with magnifying glasses, the three sleuths spent the rest of the day, most of the night, and the rest of the next day and most of that night, too, pouring over every photograph of every album.

They carefully examined each photograph for clues. They wrote the photograph's date on its back and jotted their findings in little notebooks.

Sherman spoke to Cornell just once.

"Why were you in the basement?" He leaned over an image with his strong magnifying glass and peered very closely.

"To look for a screwdriver," Cornell turned another page. "But I didn't find any."

"Nonsense, my friend," Sherman said. "The toolchests are full of screwdrivers."

Cornell yawned and picked up his magnifying glass. He was too tired to argue with Sherman, and they had too much work to do.

As they sleuthed, they asked questions about any shadows and any marks they previously blamed on poor lighting and over-exposure.

When the three sleuths finished with the photo albums, they moved from room to room, studying anything in a frame.

They napped here and there. Whenever Cornell closed his eyes, he dreamed of howls.

Dr. Wipston kept everyone's energy and spirits up with finger roast beef sandwiches and horseradish, fruit juices, relish trays with dip, and pot after pot of hot, black coffee.

And they tirelessly kept at it.

For many days and nights, they sorted and organized, noted and analyzed. At night, Cornell heard howls. No one dared to switch off the lights, not even once.

They recorded the tiniest of tiniest pinprickiest of specks, starting from earliest photos of Dr. Wipston's grandparents when they were children – when the first settlers arrived in Basketville.

They recorded the specks, the tails, the thumbprint in the bottom corner of the photo from the mayor's speech, the one he gave in the center of town just last month.

After the sleuths scrutinized the last photos, they simultaneously raised their eyes and gazed at each other in horror and disbelief.

The thing they sought had indeed been in Basketville all along.

And it was growing.

CHAPTER FIVE: WHAT BETTER THAN PRINT?

Sherman jumped up. "Sleuths: to the library!"

Cornell glanced at his wristwatch. It was nearly nine o'clock in the morning. He glanced longingly at the kitchen, and his stomach rumbled.

"What about breakfast?" Cornell whined.

"Who cares about breakfast?" Sherman returned. "We have sleuthing to do." His eyes darted over the dirty plates. "Besides, we've been eating all night." He patted his stomach. "I couldn't eat another bite."

Well, Cornell could. He stopped inside

his motor home for a few extra-large chocolate bars, which he stuffed inside his blazer pockets. Well, supernatural super sleuths needed plenty of energy to solve mysteries. So he grabbed a few orange drinks, too..

When he returned to the front sidewalk, Sherman was fidgeting on a step, and Dr. Wipston was shaking out the front porch welcome mat.

"That's very strange," Dr. Wipston said as he set the mat back into place.

"You probably forgot to put it back," Sherman snapped.

"Probably," Dr. Wipston said doubtfully. "No matter. I will get the spare."

He went inside the bungalow. Cornell unwrapped the first chocolate bar and took a big bite.

"What'd he lose?" Cornell asked around a full mouth of chocolate.

"The house key," Sharman said scornfully.

Cornel blinked. "He keeps it under the mat?"

"Where else?"

Dr. Wipston returned with the spare

key and locked the door. Then he pocketed the spare and smiled at Sherman's narrowed eyes.

"Are you quite ready?" Sherman snapped.

"Quite." Dr. Wipston smiled.

Sherman stomped off the porch and led the way to the library, his connect-the-dots book sticking out of his back pocket.

Cornell and Dr. Wipston slogged after him.

"Why are we going to the library?" Cornell asked Dr. Wipston. He fished inside his blazer for his second chocolate bar.

"To study disappearance reports. To see how far back they go. This will confirm our findings."

Fifteen minutes later, the three supernatural super sleuths reached the bustling center of town, so different from the decaying neighborhood where Sherman lived.

The library was an old, three-story stone building, very regal and very busy. Men in crisp shirts or buttoned down sweaters sat at tables looking through magazines or leaned against the shelves browsing through books.

Women in dresses, skirts, and elegant hats consulted card catalogues and brought stacks of books for checkout. A group of young children sat in the corner, wide-eyed, as a librarian read them a story. Teenagers milled in groups of two, three, and four, giggling over comic books or movie magazines.

Cornell had spent plenty of hours in this library with Sherman Homes and Dr. Wipston, conducting research into other supernatural mysteries they needed to solve. But they'd never looked through all the documentation ever documented since the beginning of Basketville. They had a long day ahead of them.

I should have brought potato chips, too, Cornell thought.

"Now, gentlemen," Sherman announced when they reached the top of the stairs. "We shall not leave until we uncover and document every single disappearance in the history of Basketville."

"I propose a more sensible plan," Dr. Wipston said. "Let's start with the Lost and Found sections of oldest newspapers and go forward. If we find disappearances since the beginning of the town's time, we need not scour them all.

"Very well," Sherman agreed. "It shall be as you say."

Cornell spent all day pouring through the microfilm that preserved the oldest editions of The Basketville Daily Journal. The Lost and Found section took up half the space.

As he read, Cornell caught snippets of conversation: "But my pen was right here!" and "It's so sad about Grandma. Her mind just went."

He read about people misplacing their reading glasses.

He read about people misplacing their school-books and their library books.

He read about people misplacing their keys, like Dr. Wipston did today.

He read about people misplacing their pocket watches and wallets and flowerpots.

He read about missing cats, missing dogs, and missing horses.

He read about missing people – and quite a few people losing their memories.

But then the "missings" grew odd.

He read about people who lost their cars. Now, maybe someone stole the cars. Maybe they forgot where they parked. But in all cases, they never saw their cars again.

It happened with furniture.

It happened with buildings.

It happened, as Dr. Wipston had said, with entire neighborhoods.

Cornell thought about Dr. Wipston's missing key. He thought about Sherman's shortened front yard. He thought about the empty lots on Bakery Drive where houses once stood – and wondered.

Thugs? Or something more sinister?

"Library closes in ten minutes," a woman's shrill voice cried.

Cornell stood and stretched. The gears in his head cranked.

He trailed behind Sherman and Dr. Wipston all the way back to 122 Bakery Drive, head down, lost in thoughts.

"Sherman," Cornell suddenly called out. "We need to talk."

But Sherman kept walking. "So talk."

"At home. Privately." He glanced hopefully at Dr. Wipston. "We could talk at dinner."

"We could." Dr. Wipston glanced back at Cornell with a weary, but kind, smile.

Sherman sighed loudly. "Very well."

Cornell wolfed through half of his stuffed pork chops, rice pilaf, sweet and sour red cabbage, and Dr. Wipston's special homemade applesauce before he asked his important question.

"Sherman." Cornell placed his elbows on the table, which is bad table manners, and leaned forward. "When did you start connecting the dots?"

"Very recently." Sherman picked up the tongs and moved another chop to his plate. "When I found my grandfather's journal."

"Journal? What journal?" Cornell threw up his hands. "You never mentioned a journal!"

Even Dr. Wipston looked surprised. "You never told Cornell about the journal?"

Sherman glanced from one sleuth to the next, clearly annoyed. "Oh, so this my fault, is it?"

"Sherman," Dr, Wipston said gently." Cornell needs all the clues if he's to help us solve the mystery."

"Very well." Sherman pushed back his chair. "I'll return shortly."

Sherman did, carrying an old,

leatherbound journal along with his connect-the-dots book.

"This." Sherman set the books on the table, "is my grandfather's journal. I found it under a floorboard in his bedroom after his death."

"Why did you pull up floorboards?" Cornell asked. "Were you looking for clues?"

"No," Dr. Wipston said. "We were remodeling the bedroom."

Cornell briefly thought of his shabby bedroom and hoped his was next.

"My grandfather lost his mind near the end of his life," Sherman said. "He destroyed the room looking for his journal. He desperately wanted it back, you see."

"That's too bad," Cornell said.

Dr. Wipston cleared his throat. "Professor, you don't understand. Sherman's grandfather didn't grow feeble in his brain. Something actually stole his mind, his memories."

Cornell dropped his fork with a loud clink.

"That's preposterous!" he exclaimed.

"No it isn't," Sherman insisted. "I've connected the dots."

He opened the journal and slipped his fingers beneath the leather. He pulled out a folded slip of unpaper and set it by Cornell, who unfolded it and sneered, "A poem?"

Sherman sniffed disdainfully. "A riddle. A rhyming riddle. His last entry said the answers are in
a place where time doesn't touch. He was worried that his deductions were disappearing. So he hid the answer in a place where it wouldn't go missing and where I could find it. This riddle was folded into the book after the final page. Read it carefully, my friend – aloud."

Curious now, Cornell did as Sherman said.

> All in a row my colors have started to fade.
> I'm best if you use me on the slowest of days.
> My face may be a little torn and my spine is a little weak.
> But underneath the outside are where my secrets like to peek.
> Don't dig too far or you might be put in your place.

*And then you're back to square one
and looking blankly at my face!*

"As I said, Professor, things are happening," Dr. Wipston said. "And they are connected."

"I believe Grandfather was close to solving the mystery," Sherman said. "So he left me this hidden clue. But I can't decipher it."

"That's simple." Cornell handed the riddle back to Sherman. "Your grandfather hid the answer in a book." Cornell stood. "We must return to the library immediately."

"But the library is closed," Dr. Wipston protested, with a glance at the window. "And it's getting dark."

Sherman slowly re-read the lines and nodded in understanding. "A book. Of course." He rose. "We must definitely return to the library."

But before they left, Dr. Wipston rechecked Cornell's wound.

"Nearly good as new," Dr. Wipston said.

CHAPTER 6: WHERE MY SECRETS LIKE TO PEEK

It was a long weary walk back to the library for the three supernatural super sleuths. For once, Cornell was too tired to protest.

But he did save the night by bringing Skelly.

For when they rounded the back of the library to the service door, Sherman and Dr. Wipston argued about the best way to enter.

Sherman wanted to look for a super-secret passageway. Dr. Wipston wanted to break the window and found just the rock for the job, too. As he raised his hand to hurl it, Skelly poked his head out of Cornell's blazer pocket, waved at the trio, and smiled a wide toothless grin.

Skelly looked like a white glow-in-the-dark skeleton toy found in cereal boxes. But he was really an expert lock-picker.

"Hi, Professor," Skelly said. "Need to get into a room?"

"Shhh." Cornell pointed to the back door.

Skelly glowed a happy green. He hopped onto Cornell's hand, He stretched his spindly fingers waaaaaay out and slid them inside the keyhole.

After a few clicks, Skelly gave Cornell the A-OK sign. Cornell turned the knob. The door swung open. Skelly jumped into Cornell's T-shirt pocket, and Cornell led the way inside.

"Sleuths let's each take a floor," Sherman announced, reclaiming his role as leader with his words. "I'll go upstairs. Dr. Wipston can take the main floor. Cornell, you head to the basement."

"The basement?" Cornell laughed. "No library sticks books in the basement."

"This library does," Sherman insisted. "They store the books for the library sale. Grandfather was always donating books. He believed in literacy, libraries, and..."

"Fine! I'll look in the basement."

As Cornell trudged toward the freight elevator, Sherman called out, "And leave no page unturned!"

"Leave no page unturned," Cornell muttered as he closed the cage and pushed the LL button.

Cornell was tired from days of unrelenting research. But he was especially tired of Sherman and his bossy ways. Sherman was no smarter than Cornell. Did Sherman get them into the library? Nope!

The clanking gears came to life. Cornell tapped his foot impatiently. "Leave no page unturned," Cornell muttered again as the elevator clanged and jerked down, down, down, down, down, down...

"Come on!" Cornell shouted.

How far down was the basement from the first floor? The center of the earth?

After what seemed like hours, the elevator stopped with a hard jolt. Cornell waited for the wobbling to stop. Every supernatural super sleuth knows it's very dangerous to leave an elevator before it is one hundred percent completely stopped.

After another long, long while, Cornell slid the caged door back and stepped into the dark basement. He switched on his ghost flashlight and pointed the beam around the room.

He noted boxes stacked to the ceiling and tall piles of random books.

He noted a stone wall to his left.

He noted a long passageway to his right.

So Cornell turned right and followed the light. He walked for a very, very, very long time. Cornell's head buzzed with exhaustion, adding to the surrealness of the journey. Finally, he reached the other side. A wooden desk, gleaming with polish and holding a shiny new electric lamp, sat near the wall. More boxes stood near the desk; these were marked "records." Moonlight from the window cast long, jagged shadows across the desk. But Cornell couldn't worry about that now. He must sort through many books. He dragged a box to the desk, collapsed onto the chair, and pulled out the first volume.

All through the everlasting night, Cornell read through book after book and reviewed piles of yellowed paper records of

Basketville's history. From time to time, the back of Cornell's neck prickled, as if someone were watching him. But Cornell saw no one, not even Sherman or Dr. Wipston.

"Cornell!"

With a yawn, Cornell opened his eyes and blinked against the strong light. He was sprawled in front of the elevator. Dr. Wipston was shining a powerful, but very ordinary, flashlight on Cornell's face. Sherman was roughly shaking Cornell's shoulder. Sherman did not look happy.

"Fine sleuth you care, sleeping on the job." Sherman tossed his head scornfully. "Dr. Wipston, you see the proof. While we slaved away on Cornell's advice, he hid in the basement to sleep."

Cornell struggled to his feet. "I didn't hide anywhere! You sent me to the basement!"

Sherman sniffed. "If you say so."

"Don't be hard on him, Sherman." Dr. Wipston cast a worried look at Cornell. "Remember, he is recovering from a leg injury." He swept his hand across the room. "Besides, Cornell only had eight books to examine. So why not nap and regain his strength?"

"Eight books!" Cornell looked up and down the length of the basement. To his left was a wall, and to his right was a wall, an empty wall, with no desk, no lamp, no window, and no stack of boxes marked "records." Just eight books stacked in two piles against the wall. Cornell shook his head. "This doesn't make sense."

Dr. Wipston gestured to the elevator. "We'd better leave. The sun is rising. Library staff will soon arrive."

The elevator quickly and smoothly ascended one floor. Soon, they were out the door and trudging home. As they walked, Cornell shared his experiences and the information he learned from the records boxes.

"Baloney," Sherman retorted. "You were dreaming."

"Maybe not," Dr. Wipston said. "Dreams don't typically provide this much detail."

They stumbled through the front door and into the kitchen. They wolfed bowls of crunchy sweetened breakfast cereal with milk without bothering to sit down. Then they tottered to their beds, even though the sun was now shining brightly.

But Cornell never fell fully asleep. He tossed, and he turned, and tossed and turned some more. He felt long shadows across his face; he heard long, wheezing howls in his ears.

Finally he kicked the covers away and wandered into the study. Sherman sat in his favorite chair, eyes drooping as he connected the dots.

"Where's Dr. Wipston?" Cornell asked.

"How should I know?" Sherman snapped.

At that moment, Dr. Wipston shouted, "Sherman! Cornell!"

Cornell met Sherman's eyes.

"The basement!" they cried in unison.

Cornell sped to the kitchen with Sherman close behind him. They flew down the stairs and over to the workbench. Dr. Wipston stoon next to the desk, a wide smile on his face.

"What?" Sherman demanded.

"The rolltop," Dr. Wipston said, still smiling.

"What about it?"

Dr. Wipston rolled back the top and

gestured.

Sherman sighed loudly. "A bunch of old invoices and dried up pens! Are you quite through?"

"Not quite."

Dr. Wipston removed the little shelf in the rolltop, which revealed another set of doors.

"Cornell, may I borrow Skelly?" Dr. Wipston asked.

Skelly poked his head out of Cornell's T-shirt pocket. "Did anyone call me?"

"Skelly, will you please open these doors?" Dr. Wipston said. "I need to see behind them."

"Certainly!"

Skelly stretched a long spindly finger and nimbly opened the lock, which revealed another set of doors. So Skelly opened those, too. Cornell and Sherman gasped.

Eight books, colors faded, spines weak, stood in a row. In a very soft voice, Dr. Wipston recited:

All in a row my colors have started to fade.

I'm best if you use me on the slowest

of days.

My face may be a little torn and my spine is a little weak.

But underneath the outside are where my secrets like to peek.

Don't dig too far or you might be put in your place.

And then you're back to square one and looking blankly at my face!

"Eureka!" Cornell whispered in excitement.

"Double that," Sherman murmured in awe.

CHAPTER 7: MAYHEM AT THE MALL

The books were the eight detective books that Sherman's grandfather wrote and published in the 1920s. All bore the name of H.J. House.

But Sherman's grandfather's name was Hector Homes.

"It's a pen name." Sherman picked up a book and flipped through the pages.

Cornell selected a book, too. As he browsed, Cornell recognized mysteries Hector had solved. He recognized Hector's writing style from his journal.

"This is brilliant," Sherman said. "If something can't be seen, it can't go missing. "But," he added impatiently, "I'm not finding any clues about dark, shadowy howls. And yet, I'm certain the clues are here."

"Oh, they are," Dr. Wipston said softly again.

Jim had removed the dust cover from one volume and was holding it out for them to see.

"Ah," Sherman murmured. "Underneath the outside..."

"Are where my secrets like to peek," Cornell finished.

Dr. Wipston nodded. "It seems Basketville was built on something that was – not good."

"Not good?" Cornell echoed.

"And what does that mean?" Sherman demanded.

Dr. Wipston cleared his throat and read.

Basketville has a strange history. From ancient times, this land was known for unearthly howling, screams in the night, and unexplained disappearances. So the land always kept changing hands. All the buyers knew was that the land seemed to be good, and the price seemed to be right. But the owners bought more than the land. They bought the curse that came with the land.

"Curse? What kind of curse?" Sherman demanded.

"Sherman, you know the answer to that." Dr. Wipston reached for another book.

"I do?" Sherman snapped. "Well, maybe my memory has gone missing."

"Listen to this," Cornell said and began to read.

My mind is starting to go. I fear other things might disappear, too. So here is all my research.

"He left us a map." Dr. Wipston held up another dust jacket. "It shows where the original deal was made."

Sherman's draw dropped. He pointed at the map. "Why that's...that's..."

"The old factory!" Cornell exclaimed.

"Yes," Dr. Wipston said. "According to Hector, no one knows who first owned the land – or who brought it from the original owners. Only the date of the very first transaction is recorded."

"Which is?" Sherman asked.

"August 13, 1666," Dr. Wipston said.

"The evilest day of all time," Sherman murmured, shaking his head and thinking deeply.

Cornell snorted. "How do you know August 13, 1666, was evilest day of all time?"

Sherman cocked his head and smirked at Cornell. "My dear, Cornell. I've connected the dots."

"Your grandfather even examined the old factory, in daylight, of course." Dr. Wipston held up another dustjacket. "But he couldn't find any information."

Sherman slid his book back into place. "Well, we need to investigate this site very thoroughly. So we must get…"

"Sherman, your grandfather already investigated that site." Cornell yawned. "I think we should take a nap."

Sherman spun around, glaring at Cornell. "We need supplies. We need to be prepared. I know just the person who can help. So let's go."

He bounded for the stairs, put his foot on the bottom step, and then turned back. "Are you coming? Or must I solve this mystery by myself?"

Dr. Wipston shut his book. "Yes, of course." He locked up the desk. He left the light on.

Cornell headed toward the stairs. "So where are we going, Sherman?"

"We're going to an incredible place that has everything we need."

"Where's that?"

"Why, the mall of course!"

Basketville Mall was just like every other indoor mall for the time. It had a food court and a movie theater, and clothing shops, and little stores that sold souvenirs, and families shopping together, and teens hanging out, and music playing not too loudly through the speakers. A sporting goods store was up ahead, and Cornell expected Sherman to turn into it. But, no, Sherman walked right past it and turned right at the hall leading to the restrooms. Dr. Wipston followed.

"I'll wait here," Cornell said, wondering why they didn't do that before they left the house. He did.

"No, you won't!" Sherman shot back. "Now hurry up!"

So Cornell heaved a big sigh and

stomped down the hall after Sherman and Dr. Wipston, mumbling unkind words about both. Sherman passed the restrooms and kept going. So did Dr. Wipston. So Cornell kept walking, too. As they walked, the walls turned to stone, and the electric lights transformed into flaming medieval torches.

When they reached the end, Sherman touched the wall, and a door opened into the largest and the most mystical, magical supply shop Cornell had ever seen. The shop had colorful stones and silver trinkets and golden medallions and powdered dragon wings and extra-long batteries and new age spices and old age seasonings and checkerboards and shoelaces guaranteed to never break. A floor sign in front of the roped-off section read, "Preferred customers only." A variety of creatures milled about the store: old wizards and young magicians, elves and goblins, other supernatural super sleuths, and even teachers at witchery schools looking for bargains and posters for their classrooms. In the background, Cornell heard a faint whirring roar, like strong winds before a storm.

Sherman grabbed a cart and wove up

and down the aisles. He picked up a bit of this and a lot of that. Then he pushed the cart to the checkout counter and laid his purchases on the conveyor belt.

The checkout clerk was a troll, with wild hair and thick glasses taped in the middle. He was munching a bologna sandwich.

"Do you have a coupon?" the troll asked.

Cornell smelled the troll's bad breath and pinched his nose.

"I do." Dr. Wipston opened his wallet.

Th troll rang up the purchases and then typed in the coupon code. "Four pombecs," the troll said.

Dr. Wipston searched among the folds. "I only have two pombecs. Sherman?"

Sherman dug into his pocket. "I have a couple dozen gold coins. Mr. Troll, do you accept two forms of payment?"

"I guess," the troll said.

The troll counted the money into the register and tore off the receipt. "Do you collect our trading stamps?"

"I do," Sherman said.

The troll laid five blue stamps onto Sherman's hand. Then he carefully stacked

Sherman's purchases into a large brown paper bag printed with zodiac symbols.

The troll then handed Sherman a thick piece of cardboard. "And here's a coupon toward your next purchase of…"

SCREAMS!!!!

"What is going on?" Sherman asked.

Loud crashes! Booms and more Booms! BANG! BANG! BANG! And RUMBLES, too. And the whine, whirr, and ROAR of a weird gale.

Cornell blinked. The troll was gone. He whirled around. Half the shelves were also gone – and so were most of the customers.

"Come on!" Dr. Wipston shouted.

Sherman grabbed his paper sack and fled, with Dr. Wipston and Cornell behind him. They ran out the door and into the hall, where the ground was now shaking, and pillars were falling, and store windows were imploding, and people were screaming and yelling, and shrieking, and crying, and running in all directions.

Dr. Wipston rushed here and there, pulling people to safety. Sherman scanned the scene, rubbing his chin and thinking. Cornell took out his little notebook and ballpoint pen to jot the clues.

But what was happening?

With each blink of Cornell's eyes, objects and people disappeared. Dr. Wipston led a man with dark glasses and a dog in a vest out of the commotion. By now, Dr. Wipston was sweating and breathing hard. So Sherman sprang into action. He ran to Dr. Wipston, pushed him against a wall, and shoved the bag into his arms.

"Stay here and hold this!" Sherman yelled. "Whatever you do, don't lose this bag!"

Then he sped into the middle of the mayhem. Cornell noted it all. The ceiling at the west end collapsed; the crowds vanished.

Suddenly, Sherman was before him.

"We've done what we can. Let's get out of here and solve this mystery! Come on, Jim!"

"Good idea," Cornell agreed. He closed his notebook, clicked his ballpoint pen to "off" and then stuffed both into his pocket.

"Oh, no!" Sherman cried. "Oh no! Oh no! Oh no! Jim! Jim, where are you? Jim?"

Cornell turned to the spot where Dr. Wipston had stood. Sherman's brown paper bag sat on the floor.

Dr. Wipston was gone.

CHAPTER 8: A CAMPIRE FIRE AND EXCUSES

By sunset, Cornell and Sherman had set up camp at the edge of the Forest of Fear and were planning their strategy.

Except this time, Cornell was doing more of the planning. Sherman was slumping in his camp chair and gazing into the fire. Cornell was heating a can of beans and trying to keep Sherman engaged.

In the distance, they still heard the wheezing howls and occasional screams.

They had not originally planned to camp. After fleeing the mall, Cornell and Sherman returned to 122 Bakery Drive to grab their gear. But more surprises awaited them. For Bakery Drive had changed again.

Less bungalows.

Less skeletal timbers and tall weeds.

Less curtains and cracked windows.

Less leaves waiting to be raked in less yards.

More missing shingles.

No more rusty fences.

As Cornell pushed open the front door, for the doorknob was now gone, too.

That's why Sherman hid the "ring the doorbell note," Cornell thought.

He stepped inside to the nearly empty parlor.

The sagging coach, the stained armchair, the threadbare carpet, the old console television, the plastic spider plant, and Sherman's fourth grade class photo were gone.

Only the plant's scuffed plastic bucket

and Jim's certificate of doctory remained.

"It lured us out," Sherman murmured. "It lured us out so it could take." He raised a fist. "I'm coming for you! You better be very afraid!"

The large oak dining room table, the lace tablecloth, and the tarnished silverware were gone. The broken dishes were strewn over the floor.

"We should leave," Cornell advised. "Before it comes back to take us, too."

So Sherman donned his sleuthing gear, gathered extra sleuthing tools, and stuffed his grandfather's journals and novels into a duffel bag. Cornell packed food and drinks from the kitchen, ignoring the missing dishes and chairs.

Then they trudged to the Forest of Fear and through it. They set up camp at its edge, in plain view of the old factory.

"This howling thing is stealing all over Basketville," Cornell said. "So the safest place is their place."

"I...I believe so," Sherman said hesitantly.

In his hurried and distraught state, Sherman had forgotten his connect-the-dots book in his study.

"If it's even still there," he said gloomily.

"We don't need it," Cornell said confidently. "You have already connected the dots."

"True," Sherman agreed. "But what good is that now? Jim is gone."

"Jim is gone for now." Cornell poured beans on a paper plate and gave them to Sherman. "But we will get Jim back. We will retrieve every item and put each where they belong."

"How?" Sherman demanded. "We still don't know what it is or where it lives."

"We know it's not good," Cornell said. "We know it's dark and howling and growing. We know it's been in Basketville since ancient times. We know it takes. It takes everything from pencils to people's minds."

"True." Sherman slowly tasted a small spoonful of beans. "But Jim…"

"Jim doesn't want you moping." Cornell ate a heaping spoonful. "So we will solve this mystery tonight." He opened a large box of cheese crackers, took a handful, and then passed the box to Sherman.

Sherman chuckled weakly.

"What's so funny?" Cornell asked.

"This." Sherman waved his hand over the scene. "Us. We're camping in plain view of the howling thing's hideout, and we're lit up by the campfire."

"To keep us safe. But it is kind of funny," Cornell agreed.

Sherman ate a little and read a little. He looked too dazed for much more. Cornell did more of the reading and eating and strategizing. But Hector House had only danced on the edge of cracking the mystery. His notes confirmed what they knew. But they didn't contain the solution. Just a large "X" in the middle of the map.

"Orange drink?" Cornell asked Sherman as he popped a can open.

"Sure."

They drank and read some more and learned nothing more. Finally Cornell closed his book, stood, and stretched.

"We're just dawdling now. We should go." Cornell checked his blazer pockets. "Did you bring the map?"

Sherman removed the jacket from the novel he was reading and held it up.

"Good. Let's find these howling not-good things and solve the mystery."

Cornell reluctantly extinguished the campfire. Never leave a fire burning unattended, his Grandpa Mo had always cautioned him. Never leave even the tiniest spark.

Sherman grabbed his paper sack of supplies. Cornell grabbed the bag of snacks and led the way across the trodden-down field to the old factory.

"You're sure we'll solve this mystery tonight?" Sherman asked.

"Yep!"

The factory was boarded up. Someone had nailed a giant wooden sign to the front: DANGER! DO NOT ENTER! Well, Cornell was not expecting to ring a doorbell and be invited inside.

Now normally Cornell would turn back. It's not safe to enter a dangerous building. But Cornell knew the greater danger was outside the building. Sometimes a supernatural super sleuth must perform dangerous tasks to solve the mystery. So only a supernatural super sleuth with the right supernatural sleuthing tools should ever tackle such a project, and Cornell only knew of three who should.

Cornell was one.

Sherman was the other.

Together, they would rescue the third.

"How are we getting in?" Sherman asked.

At that moment, Skelly poked his head out of Cornell's blazer pocket. He grinned and waved.

"Hi, Professor," Skelly said. "Need a door unlocked tonight?"

"Yep."

Skelly glowed a happy green. He hopped onto Cornell's hand, stretched his spindly fingers and frowned.

"Professor," Skelly said. "There's a big board in my way. Can you please move it?"

"If I could move it, I wouldn't need you!"

Skelly tapped Cornell's arm. "I'm a lock-opener, Professor – not a board-remover."

With that, Skelly hopped back into Cornell's pocket and burrowed himself at the bottom.

"The map shows a back entrance," Sherman said. "Maybe no one thought of boarding that door."

"It's worth a look."

Cornell opened another orange drink. Slurping loudly, he crept around the old factory with Sherman on his heels. Cornell finished his drink long before they reached the rear. Cornell didn't see a trash can, so he tossed the can onto the grass.

"You're littering?" Sherman asked, surprised.

"Only temporarily," Cornell said, "until some howling thing takes it."

"Ah! You do make a point."

They reached the back door. Skelly leaped out of the pocket and then his expression fell. The door was not boarded up. It also wasn't locked. In fact, the back of the factory had no door at all, just a black door-shaped entryway where a door should have hung.

"Why board up the front?" Cornell grumbled.

Sherman had no answer.

Cornell switched on the ghost flashlight and walked inside. But the ghost flashlight only gave the dimmest of lights. Cornell hit the side a few times. But the light never turned any brighter.

"My batteries must be going." Cornell clicked the flashlight off and on a few times. "Sherman, give me a couple."

"Oh, I didn't bring batteries."

"Fine. I guess we walk in the almost dark."

"I guess."

Cornell thought of something worse than walking in the dark. "Is this enough light to keep us from being taken?"

"Maybe. Probably."

Skelly, still hanging onto Cornell's pocket with his tiny fingers, glanced back. "I can help, Professor. Watch!"

He glowed extra hard. But Skelly's best efforts did not create light of any significance.

"It's just as well," Sherman said. "It's not a cheery place."

Cornell looked around, above, and below. Sherman was right. Cornell saw giant troughs and trolleys, giant hooks screwed into large beams near the ceiling, oversized barrels and drums, and heavy mallets, sharp knives, and giant saws with jagged teeth lined up on long tables. The entire area near the ceiling perimeter was one metal catwalk.

"What did this factory make?" Cornell asked.

"I don't know. It closed before I was born."

Cornell ripped open a bag of potato chips and offered a chip to Sherman. "Your grandfather never talked about it?"

"Never." Sherman took three chips.

They kept walking toward the center of the factory until Cornell saw something very suspicious: an extremely large X.

Skelly gasped and disappeared into Cornell's pocket.

"This must be where the original deal was made," Cornell said.

"Indeed," Sherman breathed.

As Cornell stared at the X and outlined his next move, the X began to shift.

It grew wider.

And darker.

And rounder – until it became a vast black, smoldering hole spewing sulfurous smoke.

Sherman held his breath, wide-eyed.

Cornell dropped his now empty bag of potato chips down the hole. Molten rock shot out, and Cornell jumped back and bumped into Sherman. A whirring howl filled the air, which grew into an earsplitting roar as a monstrous horde of black, dog-like creatures rushed in.

Their teeth were long and pointed.

Their eyes were flaming red.

CHAPTER NINE: WHERE IT ALL WENT BAD

The creatures sprang at them, but Sherman moved faster. He tossed his bag from the magical shop to Cornell and punched the first creature and a large POW appeared on the creature's face. He punched the second one and left a large OUCH. He ran into three with a CRUNCH and knocked several flat with a CRASH. He swung again with a BAM and a KAPOW! Then he leaped onto a cart and rolled into a row of creatures preparing to charge – KRAM!

Cornell opened Sherman's bag and pulled out a water pistol. He turned it over and over, perplexed at why Sherman bought a water pistol at a magic shop.

Finally, he pulled the trigger.

A flag with the word BANG unrolled to the ground. Five creatures fell. He pulled out a glittery wand and pointed it. Another flag unrolled – ZZZAPPPP – and a group of creatures collapsed.

"Sherman!" Cornell cried as Sherman sailed from the rafters on a large crane, knocking hundreds flat with great KLUNKS. "I don't understand!"

Cornell grabbed a sword and pointed it at creature who leaped too closely to him and – BIFF! The creature deflated.

"My friend," Sherman cried as he leaped onto a large barrel and kicked a creature away with a loud OOF! "Sometimes words hurt more than any weapon ever could!"

"Are you kidding me?"

But Sherman was climbing a ladder and kicking away the creatures that followed him with CRACKS and THWATS!

"Cornell! Do I look like I'm kidding?"

"I guess not!"

Cornell reached into his bag and pulled out a deck of cards. He threw out the first.

It landed in a puff of colored smoke: STAY BACK! Cornell threw another – more smoke and GO HOME!

The more cards Cornell threw, the thicker and blacker and smellier the smoke became. As he threw the last card, he caught a glimpse of Sherman, weary and still fighting. But not the creatures. They had doubled, no tripled, in size and number. As Sherman weakened, they strengthened.

They're feeding off him, Cornell thought. They're feeding off his energy.

And now these creatures had wrapped themselves around Sherman and were dragging him toward the hole, which was now a massive, eternal, bubbling crater.

"STOP!" Cornell yelled.

To his surprise, all the creatures froze. Sherman broke away and lunged toward Cornell, gasping, sweating, and searching out Cornell with panicked eyes.

But Cornell wasn't afraid. Of course, Cornell hadn't physically fought as hard as Sherman, But Cornell had thrown an entire deck of cards. Cornell had done plenty of thinking.

Yet while Cornell was mulling over the

situation, another surprising thing happened.

These hundreds of creatures softened, melted, and fused into one enormous, dog-like entity.

And this massive entity rose up on its hind legs and lumbered toward Cornell.

CHAPTER 10: TOP DOG

"Bad dog," Cornell scolded the gigantic creature, even though his insides were quaking. "Bad dog. Stop stealing and put everything – and everyone – back where it belongs. Right now!"

"No," the creature growled. "That's not in the contract."

Cornell wadded up the brown paper bag, stood on tiptoes, and thwapped the creature on its nose. "Bad dog!"

The creature growled again and bared

his dripping fangs.

"Oh, I know!" Cornell cried. "You're hungry! You're devouring this town one missing flowerpot at a time. But you're never satisfied. The more you take, the more you want, and the bigger and hungrier you grow! But your game is up!"

The creature threw back his head and laughed a wheezy, whirring, roaring laugh. It echoed off the walls and boomed in Cornell's ears.

"Yeah, yeah, we know," Cornell said. "You think you're so powerful. You love all this attention."

The creature smiled. "We want out."

"What do you mean – out? You are out!"

"We want all the way out. We take to make room – for us!"

"I don't care!" Sherman's voice suddenly rang out. "Bring back Jim!"

"No, MUHAHAHHAHAHAHA!"

"No, huh?" Cornell mocked.

The creature advanced.

Cornell fumbled inside all the secret, hidden pockets of his colorful blazer until he found the item he wanted. He whipped it out and waved it in front of Sherman's nose.

Sherman curled his lip back in disgust. "You really carry an empty peanut butter jar with you?"

But Cornell ignored Sherman's scorn. He was too busy unscrewing the lid. He felt the creature's hot breath on his face.

Cornell took a deep breath. He looked the creature straight into its fiery eyes.

"Well, then," Cornell said slowly. "What if...what if, we just take you?"

Sherman swiftly grabbed the creature as it let out a tornado size roar and wrenched and writhed.

But Sherman's grip was strong with the love of a longstanding friendship.

Sherman swiftly stuffed the creature into the jar; Cornell swiftly screwed on the lid.

Then Cornell flung the jar with all his might into the volcanic hole. The hole instantly swallowed the jar and vanished.

EPILOGUE

Cornell stood with Sherman at Basketville Cemetery as Sherman laid a bouquet of crimson moss-roses on the grassy grave of Dr. Jim Wipston. The headstone bore his name and the words, "Now I am quite finished."

Sherman reached into his pocket and removed a folded sheet. He handed it to Cornell and then brushed his sleeve across his eyes.

"Read it," Sherman said in a choked voice. "He knew all along."

Cornell unfolded the note and read:

My dear Sherman, while you were connecting the dots, I connected my own dots and concluded I was next. Ever since that night in the Forest of Fear, I knew this was our last adventure. The thing took something from me that night, something I can't define. I feel disconnected and out of focus. But wherever I land, I will treasure our friendship. Love cannot be taken, only given away.

Cornell returned the letter to Sherman, who slid it back into his pocket and turned to Cornell and asked, "Shall we leave? I'm famished."

"Me, too."

Soon they were back at the bungalow. Cornell headed to his room to stuff his belongings back into the garbage bag. Sherman went to the kitchen to prepare lunch.

When Cornell returned from tossing the garbage bag into the motor home,

Sherman was standing at the stove, stirring soup in a saucepan.

"I hope you like vegetable." Sherman set the spoon on a trivet and picked up a spatula. He nimbly turned the grilled cheese sandwiches to brown the other side. Then he eyed Cornell. "Well? Do you, or don't you?"

"Sure," Cornell said. "I'm just trying to get used to the sight of you actually cooking."

Sherman heaved an exasperated sigh. "Cooking isn't a mystery to me. One just follows the steps, you know. It's like…"

"…connecting the dots," Cornell finished.

"Exactly."

They talked about the next steps while they ate. Sherman planned to donate his grandfather's novels to the library but would keep the journals.

Sherman also wanted to catch up on his reading and his hobbies (fencing, boxing, and playing the violin) before the next mystery knocked on his door.

"What about you?" Sherman asked while Cornell slurped soup from his spoon. "What's next for Professor Cornell Dyer?"

"The next supernatural mystery, of

course," Cornell said, reaching for another sandwich from the platter. "Until it calls, I will relax."

Sherman reached for the teapot and refilled his cup. "He was a hero, you know," he said reflectively.

"I know." Impulsively, Cornell added, "Come with me. Leave Basketville and join me on the open road."

"What?" Sherman looked shocked. "Are you joking? Leave with you? Am I a baby that needs consoling and looking after? The idea!"

Sherman jumped up and started stacking dishes. Cornell rescued the last sandwich, took a huge bite, and shot back, "So you'll stay in Michigan forever?"

"Really, you are so tiresome. You should know by now nothing stays in one place forever."

Cornell stuffed the rest of the sandwich into his mouth and mumbled, "Goodbye, "around the bread before Sherman drafted him into drying dishes. As he left the kitchen, a glint caught his eye.

It was the glossy finish of a photograph, the one of Sherman, Dr.

Wipston. and Sherman's Uncle Teabody sitting on the front porch. The photograph was resting on the shelf where Dr. Wipston kept his cookbooks.

The image was as clear as the day Cornell took it. No, it was even more clear than that. For the wispy smudge in the bottom corner was gone.

"Sherman." Cornell picked up the photograph and held it out. "Look at this."

Sherman, hand towel slung over his shoulder, peered closely at the photograph. Then he tossed his head and returned to the sink.

"What did you expect?" Sherman asked. "We vanquished it, after all."

"We did," Cornell agreed.

Soon, Cornell was settled in the front seat, more than ready to leave Michigan behind him forever.

But before he turned the ignition, he pulled a note out of his T-shirt pocket and scanned the brief lines.

Cornell,

Thank you for all your wonderful help

over the years and for the honor of solving one last mystery with you. Please remember your promise to me the night I repaired your leg, your promise to always look after Sherman for me. He needs you now more than ever.

Jim

Cornell sighed.

Then he shrugged.

Eh, he thought. I tried.

He tucked the note back into his pocket, turned the key, and drove happily away.

One week later, Cornell was tired of relaxing. His phone was too silent, he'd run out of Wagnerian operas, and he couldn't find any good programs on his console television.

Well, if a supernatural mystery didn't come to him, he would go to it.

He went to his coat closet and pulled out a large box stuffed with paper scraps. These were all the cries for help he didn't feel like answering at the time. Cornell closed his eyes, shoved his hand through the scraps, and pulled up one: something about strange, broken toys.

Cornell reached inside his sock for his extra phone and started dialing.

THE FACTS IN THE FICTION

The characters of Sherman Homes and Dr Jim Wipston are parodies of Sherlock Holmes and Dr. Jim Watson, which British author Arthur Conan Doyle created.

The title, "The Howls of Basketville," is also parody of one of Doyle's books, "The Hound of the Baskervilles."

Sherman Homes' hobbies are similar to those of Sherlock Holmes.

The crimson-moss roses Sherman Homes laid near Dr. Jim Wipston's headstone are the same type of roses that caught Sherlock Holmes' attention in "The Adventure of the Naval Treaty."

Mr. Teabody is a parody of the cartoon character Mr. Peabody, who is an anthropomorphic dog. The cartoon character Mr. Peabody is a time-traveler and has a nephew named Sherman.

About the Author

Denise M. Baran-Unland is the author of the BryonySeries supernatural/literary trilogy for young and new adults, the Adventures of Cornell Dyer chapter book series for grade school children and the Bertrand the Mouse series for young children.

She has six adult children, three adult step-children, fourteen total grandchildren, six godchildren, and four cats.

She is the co-founder of WriteOn Joliet and previously taught features writing for a homeschool coop, with the students' work published in the co-op magazine and The Herald-News in Joliet.

Denise blogs daily and is currently the features editor at The Herald-News. To read her feature stories, visit theherald-news.com. For more information about Denise's fiction and to follow her on social media, visit bryonyseries.com.

Sue Midlock lives in Illinois with her husband and has been writing for 10 years. She started writing when the book "Twilight" first came out and fell in love with the paranormal genre.

Since then, she has written and finished her Rosewood Trilogy and just recently her anniversary edition, "Forever," which is the first book re-written for adults.

Her most recent releases are "Southern Shorts," which is an anthology of short stories about Dry Prong, Louisana and "Night Games

Timothy Baran enjoys cooking on professional and home levels. He also likes writing dark poetry and stories whose style mimics C. S. Lewis, his favorite author.

He is currently working on his first novel and a book of poetry.

But he especially loves his cat Midnight, whom he raised from a kitten.

Made in the USA
Monee, IL
28 October 2023

45354321R00069